Hey, I Love You!

For Phoebe Benwell-Froggatt, with love, of course – I. W.

For Max and Ruth – R.R.

igloo

First published 2004 by Macmillan Children's Books
This edition published 2005 by Macmillan Children's Books
a division of Macmillan Publishers Limited
20 New Wharf Road, London N1 9RR
Basingstoke and Oxford
Associated companies throughout the world
www.panmacmillan.com

ISBN: 978-1-4050-1922-4

Text copyright © IanWhybrow 2004
Illustration copyright © Rosie Reeve 2004
Moral rights asserted.

5 7 9 8 6 4

A CIP catalogue record for this book
is available from the British Library.

Printed in China

This edition © Igloo Books 2008
Cottage Farm, Mears Ashby Road, Sywell, Northants NN6 0BJ

Hey, I Love You!

Written by
Ian Whybrow

Illustrated by
Rosie Reeve

igloo

The sun was setting when Big said to Small, "I'm off to fetch supper, but just before I go, tell me the special words again."

Small had the special words ready.

> "Bolt the door
> and lock it tight,
> close the curtains
> and turn on the light.
> If I do, then I will be
> safe where the Bad Cat
> can't catch me!"

"Good," said Big. "Now, have we forgotten anything?"

Small didn't think so, so Big said goodbye.
And off he went in a hurry.

The bolt went bang.

The key went click.

Swish went the curtains
and on went the light.

And that was when
Small remembered!

He tapped on the window.
"Wait!" he called. "We *have* forgotten something!"

But Big didn't hear.

Small tapped again.

Ratatat-tat!

"Hey, Big!" he called.
"Wait! We've forgotten
something important."

But Big didn't stop.
All he could hear was the
wind in the trees.

Small thought very hard.
What should he do?

"I'll just have to be brave
and go after him," he said.
"That Bad Cat won't
catch me!"

Small ran as fast as he could.
"Hey, Big!" he called. "Wait a minute,
we forgot something important!"

But Big was too far away to hear.

Small tried again, only louder.

"Hey, *Big!*"
he squeaked.
"Wait!"

This time Big stopped.
"What was that?" he said.
"I'm sure I heard a noise.
I don't *think* it was the
Bad Cat, but I'd better hurry,
just in case."

And off went Big with a skip
and a jump – safely on his way.

Big ran along the old stone wall.

Small was still a little way behind.

"Hey!" called Small, as loud as he could. "We forgot something important!"

Big stopped again.
He listened very hard.

"I'm sure I heard something,"
he said. "I know I did.
I don't *think* it was the
Bad Cat, but I'd better
take care, just in case."

And off went Big with a skip
and a jump – safely on his way.

Big squeezed through a gap and into the barn.
There was corn enough for a month of suppers!
Big was so busy filling his sack that he didn't
hear the Bad Cat creeping up behind him.

That bad old cat
crept closer . . .

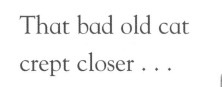

and closer . . .

and closer until . . .

What a noise!

"Yowl!" went the Bad Cat, as he fell off the cornheap and ran for his life.
"Squeak!" went Big, as he tumbled head over heels and . . .

  bumped into Small.

"What are you doing here?" gasped Big. "You know it's not safe!"

"We forgot to say *I love you*," whispered Small. And he reached up and hugged Big very tight.

Then home they dashed with their supper.

Along the wall . . .

over the stepping stones . . .

through the woods . . .

and in through their own
front door. Bang!

What a sweet yellow meal they ate that night!
"Wasn't it lucky that I had you to help me carry
the corn?" said Big. "But you really mustn't
go out on your own, not when you're so little."

"I won't," said Small, "but we never
even saw the Bad Cat, did we?"

After supper, Small was very sleepy. Big carried him to bed and tucked him safely in.

"Goodnight Small," he said. "Sleep tight." And this time, Big didn't forget.

"Hey!" he whispered.
"I love you."

Then he said it a bit
louder, just in case
Small hadn't heard.